MOONDANCE

FRANK ASCH

SCHOLASTIC INC.

New York   Toronto   London   Auckland   Sydney

ISBN 0-590-48268-8

Copyright © 1993 by Frank Asch.
All rights reserved. Published by Scholastic Inc.

12 11 10 9 8 7 6 5 4 3 2 1   5   4 5 6 7 8 9/9

Printed in the U.S.A.   23

The illustrations in this book were painted
with vinyl acrylic copolymer animation paint
on bristol board.

To Devin

One night Bear and Little Bird were sitting
outside, looking at the moon.
"You know what I wish?" said Bear. "I wish
I could dance with the moon."
"Maybe she'd like to dance with you, too?"
chirped Little Bird.

"Silly Bird," chuckled Bear. "The moon is so
  special. She wouldn't want to dance with me!"
Just then a cloud drifted in front of the moon.
"What about the clouds?" asked Little Bird.
"Would they dance with you?"
"Mmmmmm . . . maybe," said Bear.
"Why don't you ask them?"
 suggested Little Bird.

"Okay," said Bear and he called to the clouds,
"Clouds, would you come down and dance with me?"
 But the clouds stayed up in the sky.
"You see," said Bear. "Even the clouds won't come
 down to dance with me!"

Bear and Little Bird watched the sky until bedtime.

Then they said good night and went to sleep.

In the morning Bear looked out his window and
saw fog. He had never seen fog before.
"Oh, my!" he cried. "The clouds came down to
dance with me!"
Bear was so excited! He ran outside
and began to dance with the clouds.

He danced and he danced and he danced.

As the day grew warmer, the fog began to lift.

When the fog was all gone, Bear felt sad.
"Do you think I could have stepped on their toes
or something?" he asked Little Bird.
"Silly Bear," replied Little Bird. "The clouds probably
had some work to do up high in the sky, that's all."

"What kind of work does a cloud do?" asked Bear.

"Clouds make rain," answered Little Bird.

Suddenly Bear had an idea.

"Clouds," he called to the sky, "could you make
some rain for me to dance with?"

Bear heard no answer, not even a rumble of thunder.

"Oh, well," he sighed. "I have my own work to do."
Bear forgot about the clouds.
He went inside and picked up his toys.
He washed the dishes and polished
all the silverware.

When Bear was finished he looked out his window
and saw raindrops falling from the sky.
"Oh, goodie!" cried Bear and he ran outside
and began to dance with the rain!

He danced and he danced and he danced.

After a while the rain stopped.

This time Bear was not sad.
"The rain got hungry and went home
to eat supper, that's all," he said.
Bear was hungry, too.
After eating *his* supper Bear went outside
and waited for the moon to rise.

For a long time Bear gazed at the moon.
"She's so special and I'm just an ordinary bear,"
he thought. Then Bear remembered how special
it made him feel to dance with the clouds and the rain.
"Oh, Moon," he called to the sky,
"will you please come down and dance with me?"

The moon made no reply, but when Bear looked
down he saw the moon's reflection in a puddle.
"Look, Little Bird!" he cried. "The moon came
down to dance with me!"
Bear was so happy! He jumped into the puddle
and began to dance with the moon.

He danced and he danced and he danced.